Fixing the
Crack of Dawn

written by Erica Silverman • *pictures by Sandra Speidel*

Troll Medallion

Published by Troll Medallion, an imprint and trademark of Troll
Communications L.L.C.

First published in hardcover by BridgeWater Books.

Printed in the United States of America.

10 9 8 7 6 5 4 3 2 1

Library of Congress Cataloging-in-Publication Data

Silverman, Erica.
Fixing the crack of dawn / by Erica Silverman; pictures by Sandra Speidel.
p.   cm.
Summary: Surrounded by the desert animals that live near her home, Lisa
searches for the crack of dawn so that she can fix it.
ISBN 0-8167-3458-5 (lib. bdg.)   ISBN 0-8167-3459-3 (pbk.)
[1. Deserts – Fiction.   2. Animals – Fiction.   3. Morning – Fiction.]
I. Speidel, Sandra, ill.   II. Title.
PZ7.S58625Fi   1994   [E] - dc20   93-33807

*To Zoe and Zia, who awake me each morning
at the crack of dawn with hugs and kisses. —S.S.*

To my Mima—alive in my heart. —E.S.

Lisa watched from her bedroom window as the desert sun went down.
Darkness spread like a blanket over cactus, tree, and brush.

"Time to sleep." Papa tucked Lisa in with a hug. "Mama will be home
early tomorrow morning."

"How early?" Lisa asked.

"At the crack of dawn," said Papa.

What was the crack of dawn? Lisa closed her eyes. Was it big or little?
Was it narrow or wide? Was it on the ground or in the sky? She
pictured a long, jagged line stretching from her front yard up into the
clouds.

   "Is there really a crack?" she asked. But when she opened her eyes,
Papa had already disappeared down the hall.

Lisa pushed off the covers. She slipped into her brother's room.

"Roy," she whispered. "What's the crack of dawn? Is it dangerous?"

Roy looked up from the game he was playing. He rolled his eyes. "It's bad, very bad," he replied. "If dawn cracks, watch out."

Lisa bit her lip. "What will happen?"

"Well…" Roy stopped to think. His eyes gleamed. "For one thing, the sun won't be able to come up."

"Then how can the day begin?" Lisa asked.

"Could be a problem." Roy nodded.

"Shouldn't we fix it?" asked Lisa.

"You could try glue," said Roy. And he shrugged.

"Will you help me?" asked Lisa.

"No way. I hate getting up early. Anyway, shouldn't you be in bed?"
He looked up. "Dad, Lisa's bugging me," he yelled.

Lisa glared at her brother.

"Lisa!" her father called. He came into the room. He took her hand and walked her back to bed. "I know you miss Mama when she has to travel for work. But the sooner you fall asleep, the sooner you'll see her."

Lisa tugged at his arm. "But Roy said…"

"Shhh. Sleep." Papa kissed her good night.

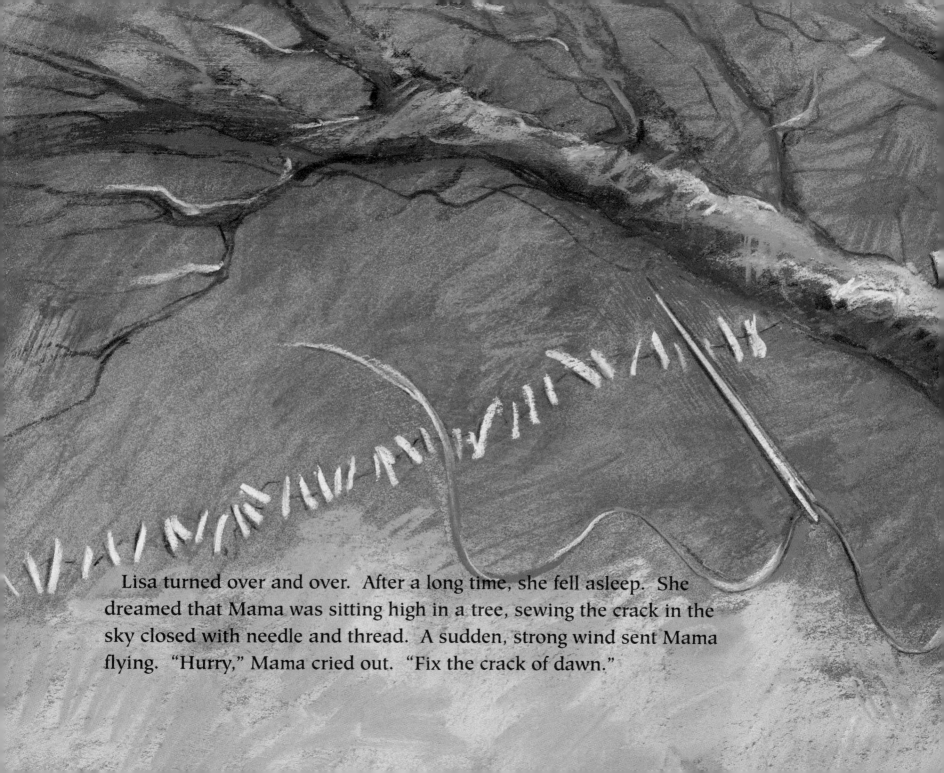

Lisa turned over and over. After a long time, she fell asleep. She dreamed that Mama was sitting high in a tree, sewing the crack in the sky closed with needle and thread. A sudden, strong wind sent Mama flying. "Hurry," Mama cried out. "Fix the crack of dawn."

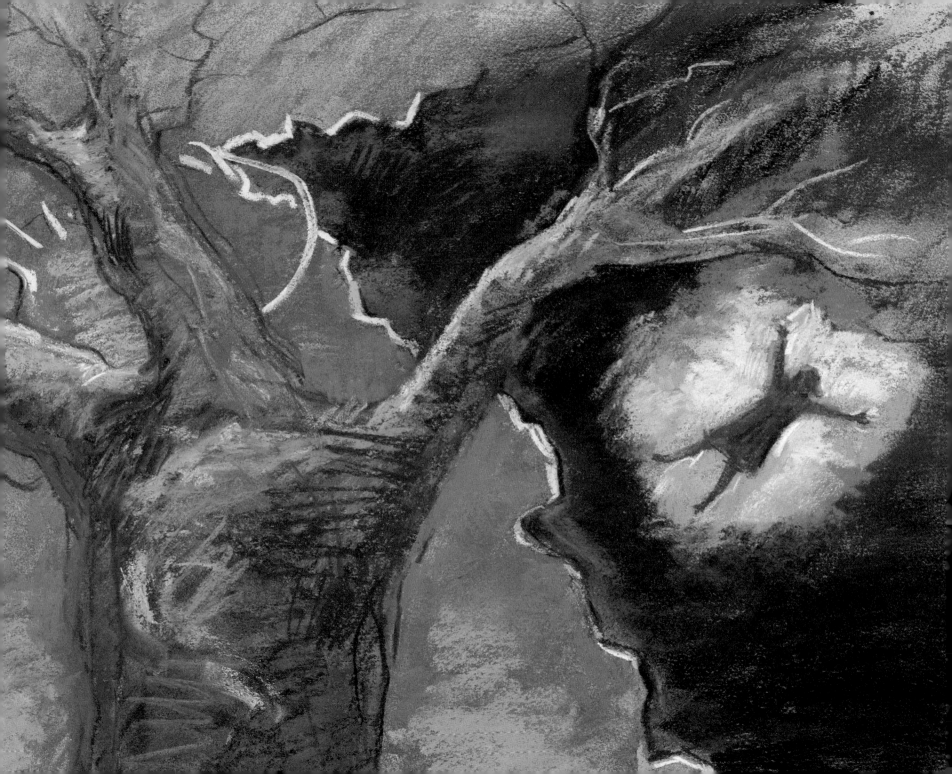

Lisa woke up. I *will* fix it, she decided. Even if I have to do it myself.
She took a tube of glue from her art box.

Outside, she shivered in the cool, inky darkness. She listened to the
click, click, click of the cicadas. An owl hooted. Wings rustled overhead.
Joshua trees stood like giants, their twisted arms reaching for the moon.
The scent of desert flowers sweetened the air.

But where was the crack of dawn?

Slowly, Lisa walked along the side of the house. Wasn't that a crack, there on the porch wall? It was so small she could barely see it.

A lizard darted by.

"Maybe the crack of dawn starts small," Lisa said to the lizard. "But what if I can't find it before it gets too big?"

The lizard stood still. It raised its head sideways and blinked.

"I have to fix it so the sun can come up, so the day can begin, so Mama can come home," Lisa explained.

The lizard flicked its tail and darted away.

Lisa bit her lip. She hurried into the front yard. The sky was fading to a bluish gray.

"Ouch." Lisa scraped her knee on a big rock. Wasn't that a crack, there in the rock? It was so wide she could fit both her hands inside it.

A tortoise lumbered out from behind a mesquite thicket.

"Maybe the crack of dawn is very wide," Lisa said to the tortoise. "What if I don't have enough glue?"

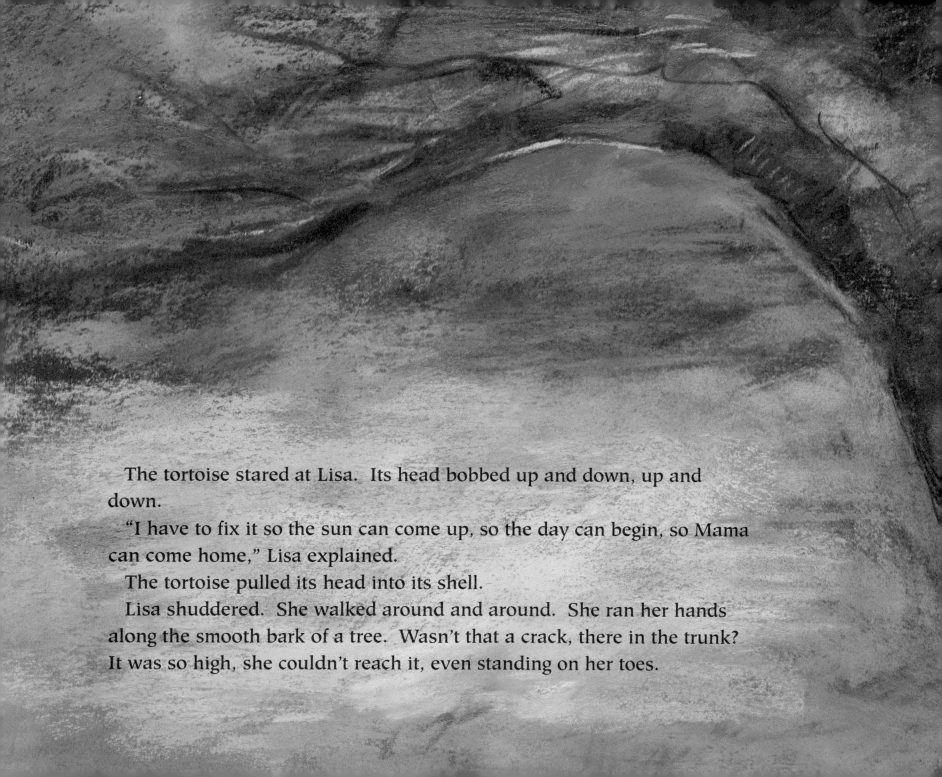

The tortoise stared at Lisa. Its head bobbed up and down, up and down.

"I have to fix it so the sun can come up, so the day can begin, so Mama can come home," Lisa explained.

The tortoise pulled its head into its shell.

Lisa shuddered. She walked around and around. She ran her hands along the smooth bark of a tree. Wasn't that a crack, there in the trunk? It was so high, she couldn't reach it, even standing on her toes.

A roadrunner hopped onto a tree stump.

"Maybe the crack of dawn starts way up high," Lisa said to the roadrunner. "What if I can't reach it?"

The roadrunner stood still. Its eyes flitted from side to side.

"I have to fix it so the sun can come up, so…"

Lisa stopped. Why was everything so still?

Nothing moved. The owl stopped hooting. Even the cicadas were quiet.

Something was about to happen. But what?

The yard and the hills beyond seemed to shimmer in a light blue haze. It wasn't dark. It wasn't light. It wasn't day. It wasn't night.

Lisa looked up.

Pink streaks brushed across the pale blue sky. Lit from behind, shifting clouds glowed yellow and red, orange and violet.

And then, from one side to the other, stretched a thin, bright line of orange light.

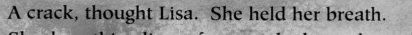

A crack, thought Lisa. She held her breath.

Slowly, a thin sliver of sun peeked out above the crack. Higher and higher it rose, until it shone full and round in the sky.

"Oh," Lisa whispered. She dropped the tube of glue. And she opened her arms wide to greet the sun.

The roadrunner raised its tail, puffed out its feathers, and cooed. The tortoise started to dig a hole in the sand to hide from the day's heat. The lizard crawled onto a rock.

A car rumbled up the road and pulled into the driveway.

"Mama!" Lisa jumped into Mama's arms.
Mama twirled her around and around.
Lisa pointed to the sky. "Mama, I saw it. I saw the crack of dawn."
Mama smiled. "Magical, isn't it? This is my favorite time of day."

Lisa sighed. "Mine, too." She stared at the sky. "But Roy said…"
She stopped.

"What did Roy say?" asked Mama.

Lisa thought for a minute. Then she shrugged. "Oh, nothing. He was
just teasing me."

And she took Mama's hand and hurried inside to tell Papa and Roy all
about the crack of dawn.